Just the Way I Am

SEAN COVEY

Illustrated by **Stacy Curtis**

Ready-to-Read

Simon Spotlight

New York   London   Toronto   Sydney   New Delhi

To my daughter Victoria (a.k.a. Elle).
I love you just the way you are,
full of life and oozing with proactivity.
—Sean Covey

For my beautiful wife, Jann—I love you
just the way you are.

—Stacy Curtis

SIMON SPOTLIGHT
An imprint of Simon & Schuster Children's Publishing Division
1230 Avenue of the Americas, New York, New York 10020
This Simon Spotlight edition November 2019
Copyright © 2009 by Franklin Covey Co.
For information about special discounts for bulk purchases, please contact Simon & Schuster
Special Sales at 1-866-506-1949 or business@simonandschuster.com.
Manufactured in the United States of America 0719 LAK
2 4 6 8 10 9 7 5 3 1
Library of Congress Cataloging-in-Publication Data
Names: Covey, Sean, author. | Curtis, Stacy, illustrator.
Title: Just the way I am / by Sean Covey ; illustrated by Stacy Curtis.
Description: First Simon Spotlight paperback edition. | New York : Simon Spotlight, 2019. | Series:
Ready-to-read. Level 2 | Series: The 7 habits of happy kids ; 1 | Originally published by
Simon & Schuster Books for Young Readers in 2009. | Summary: When Biff the beaver makes fun of
Pokey's quills, his friends help the porcupine feel a lot better about himself.
Includes note to parents and discussion questions.
Identifiers: LCCN 2019017113 | ISBN 9781534444447 (paperback) | ISBN 9781534444454 (hardcover) |
ISBN 9781534444461 (eBook)
Subjects: | CYAC: Teasing—Fiction. | Schools—Fiction. | Self-esteem—Fiction. | Porcupines—Fiction. |
Animals—Fiction. | BISAC: JUVENILE FICTION / Readers / Beginner. | JUVENILE FICTION / Imagination &
Play. | JUVENILE FICTION / Social Issues / Self-Esteem & Self-Reliance.
Classification: LCC PZ7.C8343 Ju 2019 | DDC [E]—dc23
LC record available at https://lccn.loc.gov/2019017113

Pokey Porcupine was sad.

Every time Pokey walked by Biff,
Biff made fun of him.
"Hey, Pokey. Your quills look like
a pile of toothpicks," said Biff.

Pokey would go home
and look in the mirror.
He said, "Biff is right.
My quills look funny.
I'm not going
to school anymore."

His friends tried to help.
"I like your spiky quills,"
said Goob Bear.
"Biff is being outlandish,"
said Sophie Squirrel.

"Out-what?"
said Sammy Squirrel.
"It means silly," said Sophie.
"There's nothing wrong
with your quills."

"You're a porcupine—
you're supposed to have quills,"
said Jumper Rabbit.
"Just like I'm a rabbit—
I'm supposed to be bouncy."

Pokey went for a walk
in the meadow.

He remembered
what his friends had said.

He stopped and looked
at his reflection in Cherry Creek.

He wiggled his quills up.

He wiggled his quills down.
They made a nice tinkly sound
in the wind.

They sparkled in the sun.
Pokey decided that
his quills weren't so bad.
"I like myself
just the way I am,"
he said.

The next day,
Pokey went back to school.

"How come your quills
poke out so far?" said Biff.

Pokey was not going to let Biff
ruin his day.

He smiled and walked away.

The next morning, Pokey decided
he liked his quills so much
he would show them off at school.

All of Pokey's friends
gathered around him.

Pokey loved his quills.
Everyone loved his quills.
"I wish I had quills," said Biff.

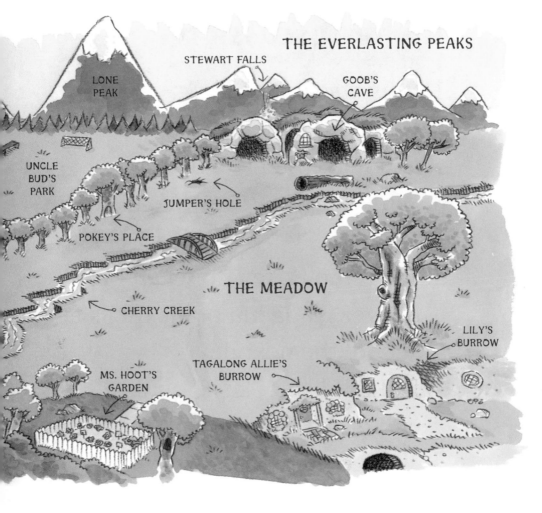

Up for Discussion

1. Why was Pokey sad?
2. What did Pokey's friends do to try and make him feel better?
3. What helped Pokey like his quills again?
4. What did Pokey do when Biff Beaver made fun of his quills at school the next day?
5. Did Biff like Pokey's quills at the end of the story? What made Biff change his mind?
6. Has anyone ever said something to you that hurt your feelings? What did you do about it? Who is in charge of being happy or sad?

Baby Steps

1. The next time someone makes fun of you, smile and walk away, just like Pokey did.
2. Name three things you like about yourself.
3. Tell your mom or dad one thing you want to get better at, like drawing pictures or brushing your teeth.
4. If you hurt someone's feelings, like a friend or a brother or sister, make sure you tell them you're sorry.

PARENTS' CORNER

HABIT ① —Be Proactive: *You're in Charge*

I remember when my daughter didn't want to go to school because some girl made fun of her freckles, or the time my son became self-conscious about his ears after a friend called him Dumbo. Ouch! The fact is, our kids are going to hear negative comments about themselves from time to time. We can't stop it from happening, but we can prepare them for it by teaching them that they do have a choice. They can let rude comments ruin their day, or they can ignore them and replace them with positive self-talk. This doesn't mean that negative comments won't hurt. They always do. Learning to be the master of our moods and to carry our own weather is one of the great challenges of life, even for adults. But that is exactly what it means to be in charge of your own life, or to be proactive, which is the first habit of happy kids. We can't control what others say or do to us. But we can control what we do about it. And that is what counts. As Eleanor Roosevelt put it, "No one can make you feel inferior without your consent."

In this story, point out how all of us will have a bully like Biff or sometimes even a friend say something hurtful. And we can choose to let it bring us down or choose to shake it off, like water off a duck's back. In the end, Pokey made a good choice—he listened to his friends and his heart instead of listening to Biff.